The Yoyo and the Piggy Bank

By Susan Werner Thoresen
Illustrated by Keith Eveland

PETER E. RANDALL PUBLISHER
Portsmouth, New Hampshire
2015

ISBN: 978-1-942155-05-8

Library of Congress Control Number: 2014958922

Published by

Peter E. Randall Publisher

Box 4726

Portsmouth, NH 03802

www.perpublisher.com

Book design by Grace Peirce

Contents

1. The Yoyo

Anna and her friend Jackson were playing outside. Jackson showed Anna his new toy, a glow-in-the-dark, bright green yoyo. Jackson made the yoyo go down and back up the string.

He said, "I'm so glad to have this yoyo. I want to learn tricks. Would you like to try it, Anna?"

"Yes!" smiled Anna. She put her middle finger through the glowy, bright green yoyo's string loop. Then she let go of it. "Look, Jackson, the yoyo went down but only came part way up."

"Go ahead and try again," said Jackson.

"Thanks. It's hard to do! I wish I had my own yoyo," she said.

At lunch, Anna told her mom about it.

"Guess what?" she asked. "Jackson let me try his new, bright green, glowy yoyo. It's fun to play with it. Can I have one?"

"Hmm," said Anna's mom as she gave her a hug. "How much does a yoyo cost? When I was a little older than you, I got a wooden yoyo for my birthday. I loved learning different tricks."

After lunch, Jackson came over to Anna's house. He brought his glowy, green yoyo.

"Where did you get that yoyo?" Anna asked.

"It was a birthday gift," he said. "Now I want to learn some tricks."

"May I try it?" Anna's mom asked. "I wonder if I can still *walk the dog*."

"What's that?" asked Anna.

"Watch," her mom said. She put Jackson's yoyo on her finger. She sent it down to the floor. The yoyo hit the floor and then rolled across it. Then it came back to her hand.

"Wow!" said Anna and Jackson.

"I didn't know my mom knew how to use a yoyo!" Anna said.

2

2. Mr. Jones's General Store

Anna's mom needed to get some groceries. "Anna and Jackson, would you like to go to Mr. Jones's General Store?" she asked.

"Oh, yes," said Anna. "Maybe his store has yoyos."

"I'll have to ask my mom first," said Jackson. "May I call her on the phone?"

"Certainly," said Anna's mom.

Jackson's mom said it was OK, so they all walked to the store.

Mr. Jones's General Store was filled with many different items. The store had fresh fruit. It had frozen food. There were big brooms. The store also had terrific toys. Anna and Jackson found a large box of yoyos. They had different colors: orange with a gold swirl, sky blue, pink with a silver swirl, silver, lemon yellow, cloud white, and sparkly, fancy purple.

"How much is a yoyo, Mr. Jones?" asked Anna.

"Five dollars," said Mr. Jones. "What color would you like? Would you like to buy one?"

"Yes, but I don't have any money," said Anna. "I really like that sparkly, fancy, purple yoyo. It's beautiful."

"I already have a yoyo," said Jackson. He showed Mr. Jones his glow-in-the-dark, bright green yoyo.

"I see you know how to work it," said Mr. Jones. Then he took a cardinal red yoyo out of his pocket. "Do you know how to *rock the cradle*?"

"No! Can you show us?" Jackson asked.

Mr. Jones rolled his cardinal red yoyo down the string. He grabbed the string with both hands and made a triangle. The yoyo swung back and forth, just like a cradle.

"Wow! That looks hard!" said Jackson.

"Yes," said Anna, "but when I get my yoyo, I bet Mr. Jones and my mom can teach us."

4

3. What Can Anna Do?

"Anna, do you think you could earn the money to buy a yoyo?" asked her mom.

"How can I earn money?" asked Anna.

"Well, Anna, think about it. What can you do to help?" asked her mom.

"Oh! I can sweep the floor and vacuum. I can take out trash. I can rake the leaves. I can water and weed gardens. You're right. I can do many things," said Anna.

Jackson said, "I'd like to help you get that yoyo so we can yoyo together. I walk Mr. Clemens's dog, Zoe, for him when he's at work. Do you want to help?"

"Thanks, Jackson, but I think I should earn the yoyo money by myself," said Anna.

Jackson said, "OK. Maybe there is some other way you can help with Zoe to earn money. If you want to help me, meet me at Mr. Clemens's house at three o'clock."

Then Jackson went home for a snack.

4. Who Needs Help?

Anna's mom said, "Are there any other neighbors who need help?"

"Yes, Ms. Lilli," said Anna. "She broke her leg bike racing and is on crutches."

"Why don't you visit Ms. Lilli and bring her some cookies?" said her mom. "You could ask if there is anything you can do to help."

"Great idea," said Anna.

Anna went to Ms. Lilli's house and knocked on the door. "I brought you some chocolate chip cookies. I hope you like them," smiled Anna.

"How wonderful. I love chocolate chip cookies," said Ms. Lilli. "It's very hard to cook and clean when you have a leg cast and use crutches."

"Would you like me to help clean? I can sweep the floors and I can empty the trash. I am earning money to buy a fancy, sparkly, purple yoyo," Anna said.

"What a wonderful idea, dear. You would be a big help. The broom and dust pan are in the closet," smiled Ms. Lilli.

Anna swept the floor. She took out the trash and put the cans and bottles into the recycling bin. Then Anna washed her hands and got Ms. Lilli a glass of milk to go with her cookies.

"Thank you for your help, Anna. I'd like to pay you two quarters," said Ms. Lilli.

"You're welcome, but you don't have to pay me. I'm glad to help," said Anna.

"Nonsense, Anna. I want to help you get that fancy, sparkly, purple yoyo," said Ms. Lilli. "Please take the 50 cents."

"All right. Thanks so much. The yoyo costs five dollars and these are my first quarters." Anna was proud she earned 50 cents all on her own. She skipped all the way home.

5. The Piggy Bank

"Look, Mom. Ms. Lilli gave me two quarters for helping her! How many quarters do I need to buy the yoyo?" Anna asked.

"Twenty quarters," replied her mom. "Four quarters make a dollar. Five stacks of four quarters make 20 quarters—and that's five dollars. You've made a good start."

"Where can I keep the money so I don't lose it?" asked Anna.

"I have just the thing, something very special," said her mom. "Come with me."

They went to the closet. Her mom got a box from the top shelf. "Here, Anna, this is for you," she said.

Anna opened the large box.

"This was your grandfather Baba's humongous, pink piggy bank," said Anna's mom. "He wanted you to have it when you were old enough to save money. Today you've started saving, so this is a good day to give it to you."

Anna hugged her mom. She was very pleased. "Boy, Baba did have a humongous, pink piggy bank! It's so cute. It will hold lots of coins. Thank you for saving it for me. I really like it," said Anna.

"You can drop your two quarters into the bank to save them," said her mom. "Baba gave me a special key for the bank. When you have saved enough money, we'll use the key to open it. Baba liked to save money and shake his bank when he added to it."

Anna put the two quarters into the bank and shook it. It made a nice little *pinging* sound like a baby rattle.

"Now I need to earn 18 more quarters," said Anna.

$.25 + $.25 = $.50 total

6. Jackson and the Dog

"Mom, it's almost three o'clock. Would it be OK if I helped Jackson walk Zoe, Mr. Clemens's dog? There may be other jobs I can do there," said Anna.

"Go ahead," her mom said. She gave Anna a hug. Mr. Clemens lived at the end of their street and had a fenced yard. In the yard was Zoe's doghouse. Jackson was already there when Anna arrived.

"I'm glad you came, Anna," said Jackson. "Mr. Clemens asked me to clean Zoe's doghouse today. I could use your help."

"I hope Zoe's doghouse isn't too dirty! Let's do it!" said Anna.

Jackson got the hose and a bucket. Anna got a sponge, soap and a brush. Anna put the soap in the bucket. Jackson added the water. First, they washed the outside of the doghouse. Next, they brushed out the inside. There were a lot of dog hairs.

"Zoe's doghouse looks great," said Anna.

After cleaning up, Jackson said, "It's time to take Zoe for a walk. Here, Zoe, let me put this leash on." Zoe wagged her tail. She was happy to go for a walk.

Anna, Jackson and Zoe walked around the block. Zoe stopped to smell the roses. She stopped to visit the trees. She tried to chase a squirrel. Soon they got back to Zoe's house. Mr. Clemens was home from work. Zoe wagged her tail and jumped up on Mr. Clemens.

"Hi, Zoe! You had a nice walk, I see! That was a very good job cleaning the doghouse. I'm glad you put all the cleaning supplies away. Did Anna help you, too?" asked Mr. Clemens.

"Yes, Mr. Clemens. Anna helped me," said Jackson. "She's trying to earn money for a yoyo like mine."

"That's a good idea, Anna. Cleaning the doghouse is a big job, and you both did it well. I'm going to give both of you a dollar coin *and* a half-dollar coin," said Mr. Clemens. "A half-dollar is 50 cents, the same as two quarters. So a dollar plus a half-dollar makes six quarters."

"Wow! Thank you, Mr. Clemens," said Anna. "I've never seen dollar or 50-cent coins."

"Did you know each coin has *Liberty* and the year it was made on it?" Mr. Clemens asked. "The half-dollar coin honors the 35th president, John F. Kennedy."

"My dollar coin has a woman on it and says 1979. The half-dollar says 2000," said Anna.

"Mine say 2003 and 1999. Look, my dollar coin is different and has a woman with a baby on it," said Jackson.

"Anna, your dollar coin honors Susan B. Anthony, who for 70 years worked to get African Americans and women equality and the right to vote. The 19th 'Anthony' Amendment passed in 1920.

"Jackson, your coin honors Sakajawea, a Native American who carried her baby Jean and guided the Lewis and Clark Expedition from 1804 to 1806 exploring the northwestern United States," said Mr. Clemens.

"Thanks for the coins, Mr. Clemens."

Mr. Clemens said, "You're welcome. Both of those coins equal a dollar bill. I know what Anna wants to buy, but what about you, Jackson?"

Jackson said, "I am saving to get a birthday present for my mom."

"Thanks, Jackson, for letting me help you," said Anna.

"It made cleaning the dirty doghouse fun," said Jackson.

7. Quiet Time

Anna went home.

"Look, Mom. Mr. Clemens gave Jackson and me each a dollar and a half-dollar for cleaning Zoe's doghouse. They are different than quarters," Anna said.

"Yes, but they equal six quarters. When you add them to your two quarters, you have eight quarters. That's two dollars," said her mom. "When you get two more quarters, you'll be halfway to getting your five-dollar yoyo."

Anna put her dollar and 50-cent piece in the piggy bank. She shook the piggy bank. "Can you hear that sound?" she asked her mom.

$.50 + $1.50 = $2.00 total

Her mom said, "Yes, your humongous, pink piggy bank jingles a little louder with four coins. What color yoyo do you want?"

"Not green. I want something different than Jackson. I really, really like that fancy, sparkly, purple yoyo at Mr. Jones's General Store," said Anna. "The pink yoyo with the silver swirls is awesome, too."

"Those are both good choices. Why don't you draw a picture of you and a yoyo? See what color you choose," said her mom.

"OK," said Anna. She was happy to take a break. Tomorrow she could do more.

8. Grampa and His Leaves

The next morning, Anna looked out her window and saw Grampa was outside. "Mom, may I go visit Grampa? He's in his rocking chair on his front porch."

"Yes. Would you like to bring him a snack?"

"Sure. Do we have any donuts? Grampa loves donuts," said Anna.

"Look in the cupboard and see what you can find," said her mom.

Anna found the donuts and put them on a plate. Then she carefully walked down the street, happy to visit Grampa. When she got there, she asked, "Would you like some donuts? Do you need any help in your yard?"

Grampa smiled and said, "Thanks for the donuts. You know that's my favorite snack in the morning. Your mom told me you are earning some money to buy a yoyo. I always like your help. Would you like to rake the lawn?"

"Yes," said Anna. "Did she tell you I've already earned two dollars?"

He said, "Wow. That's a great start. Anna, you can get the rake and leaf bag in the garage."

It took a long time to rake the lawn. There were a lot of leaves. Grampa sat in his rocker on the porch and ate a donut. He watched and rocked back and forth. Anna made a big pile of leaves.

"Grampa, would you like to jump into the pile of leaves?" she asked.

Grampa was surprised. He hadn't jumped into a pile of leaves since he was a kid.

"Sure!" he said.

He came down from the porch and jumped right into the piles of leaves. Then Anna jumped. They had leaves all over their hair and clothes. They both laughed.

"That was an epic jump," said Anna.

"Let's do it again!" said Grampa.

Grampa helped Anna rake the pile big again. Anna went first. She jumped. Then Grampa lay down on the lawn. He rolled into the pile like a log.

"Grampa, you look pretty funny," laughed Anna.

"So do you! That was fun," said Grampa.

Then Anna raked up the leaves. Grampa held open the leaf bag. Anna filled the bag with leaves.

When Anna was done, Grampa gave her a kiss on the forehead.

He said, "You did a good job, and we had fun. I'm glad to see you didn't quit a hard job. I'd like to give you some money for a special treat. Here are five dimes and two quarters. Thank you for your help. Do you still want a yoyo?"

"You're welcome, Grampa. Oh yes, I'd like a beautiful, fancy, sparkly, purple yoyo. Thank you for the dimes and quarters. I don't have any dimes. I think five dimes equal 50 cents, so don't five dimes and two quarters add up to one dollar?"

"Yes, indeed. You're a smart girl to figure that out," said Grampa. "Did you see the quarters have different states on the back?

"Look, our state is on one!" said Anna. "The yoyo costs five dollars. Now I have saved three dollars. I only have to get two more!"

"I'm glad you're saving money for something special," said Grampa. He thought about what fun they had and watched her run home.

9. Corn Bread and Honey

Anna put the five dimes and two quarters in the big pink piggy bank.

"Mom," she called, "Now I have a dollar, a half-dollar, four quarters, and five dimes in the piggy bank. All I need is eight more quarters to make five dollars." She shook the piggy bank by her mom's ear. "Can you hear that money?" Anna asked.

"Oh! It sounds like a lot of money," said Anna's mom.

"It is! I really like to shake the piggy bank," said Anna. "It sounds different each time I add money. This time it is much louder."

Anna's mom gave her a hug. "While you were at Grampa's, I made corn bread. Would you like some with honey?" she asked.

"Yummy. I love corn bread and honey. Can Jackson come over to have a piece with us?"

"Certainly, that would be nice."

Jackson was outside using his bright green yoyo. He was getting better making it go *around the world* in a circle. He tried the *walk the dog* trick like Anna's mom, but it was harder to do.

Anna wished she had a yoyo just then.

$1.00 + $2.00 = $3.00 total

"Would you like a piece of corn bread with honey, Jackson?" asked Anna. "My mom made it when I was raking leaves. Maybe she could do that *walk the dog* trick for us again."

"Thanks. I love corn bread," said Jackson. After they quickly ate the delicious corn bread, they both licked their fingers clean. Jackson didn't want to get honey on his green yoyo.

"Guess what?" said Anna. "I only need to earn two more dollars to get my fancy, sparkly, purple yoyo."

"Nice going. Here, Anna. Would you like to try mine?" asked Jackson.

"OK, I'll try it," said Anna. "Oh no! I can make the yoyo go down, but it doesn't always come all the way back up!"

"It takes practice. It took me a while, too," said Jackson.

Anna's mom said, "Don't worry. It took me a while to learn yoyo tricks, too. I'll show you both how to *walk the dog* and maybe another cool trick when Anna gets her fancy, sparkly, purple yoyo."

10. The Piano Teacher

The next day, Anna looked out the kitchen window. Her next-door neighbor, Ms. Avery, was walking home. She had two huge bags of groceries and her purse in her hands. Anna raced outside. "Ms. Avery, do you need any help carrying in your groceries and putting them away?" she asked.

"Thank you very much, dear," Ms. Avery said. "What a kind girl you are to offer to help." She handed Anna a bag of groceries. They were heavy.

Anna carried the groceries into Ms. Avery's kitchen. She knew just what to do. She put the ice cream into the freezer. She put the milk into the refrigerator. She put the cereal and crackers into the cupboard.

"Anna, here is a bowl. Please put the fruit into this bowl and leave it on the counter," said Ms. Avery. Anna put the apples, oranges and bananas in the bowl.

"You're a big help, Anna. You put all the groceries away. Thank you."

Anna said, "You're welcome. Before I go, could we play the chopsticks duet you taught me at my piano lesson last week?"

Ms. Avery was very pleased Anna remembered the duet, so they sat down together at the piano and played the song.

24

"Anna, you played that really well. Aren't you trying to save some money for something special? Let me find my purse so I can give you some money for helping me."

"Oh yes, I want to buy a fancy, sparkly, purple yoyo. It costs five dollars, and I have already earned three dollars. I'm putting the money I earned in my humongous, pink piggy bank!"

"Here are two quarters," said Ms. Avery. "Do make sure you visit me with your new, purple yoyo next time. Maybe we can play a duet again, too."

Anna walked back home and put her two quarters in her big piggy bank and shook it so all the coins rattled around. Hearing that rattling noise made Anna happy.

"Mom, now I only need to earn six more quarters."

$.50 + $3.00 = $3.50 total

11. The Rainy Day

The next day, it was rainy. Anna asked, "Mom, is there something special you would like me to do?"

Her mom thought and said, "Certainly. I am going to clean the kitchen cupboards. Would you like to help me?"

"What would I do?" asked Anna.

"You could clean the two cupboards with the food. I will do the cupboards with the dishes and glasses."

"I can do it," Anna said. She wondered if her mom was going to pay her.

Anna's mom appeared to read her thoughts. She said, "I'm glad you didn't ask me to pay you. You are a member of the family. Family members are expected to help and not be paid. I know you want to earn money for the yoyo. That should be earned in other ways."

Anna swallowed hard and said, "I know." Even so, she wished her mom would pay her to help!

All morning, Anna and her mom cleaned, one cupboard at a time. Anna emptied the food cupboards. She cleaned them and then put almost everything back.

She found yucky things like a dead fly. She did not put that back! She found her favorite foods like peanut butter, honey and jelly. She found the ingredients to make chocolate chip cookies!

At the back of the second cupboard, she found a little blue pot with a lid. It was hidden behind the cereal.

"Mom, look what I found! What's in this blue pot?" asked Anna.

"Why don't you take off the lid and see?" said her mom.

Anna emptied the blue pot on the counter top. Out came a bunch of coins.

"Let's count them," said her mom.

"I count 15 coins. The quarters have different states. Why are the pennies a different color?" asked Anna.

"Pennies are made from copper," said her mom. "It takes 25 pennies to make one quarter."

"Look, there is a dime. Is that the same as ten pennies?" asked Anna.

"Yes."

"Mom, I count five quarters, four dimes, five pennies and something else," said Anna. "What's that silvery coin with the building on one side and a man on the other?"

"That is Thomas Jefferson on a nickel. He was the third president. A nickel is equal to five pennies," said Anna's mom. "Here is a quarter. What else makes 25 cents?"

Anna made a pile of two dimes and one nickel. Then she took away the nickel. Anna replaced it with five pennies.

"Very good," said her mom. "Did you know five nickels equal one quarter, too?"

"I know," said Anna. "Why is the dime smaller than the nickel? The dime is worth twice as much."

"That's a good question. The next time we go to the library, we'll look that up or we can use the Internet," said her mom. "The money in the pot adds up to one dollar and 75 cents. That's the same as seven quarters."

Anna put the money back in the blue pot and the pot back in the cupboard. Then she finished cleaning the cupboards.

12. A Special Occasion

Anna's mom was very pleased with the clean kitchen. She fixed a lunch of carrots, a peanut butter and jelly sandwich, milk and two chocolate chip cookies. She put the little blue pot with the money on the table. After eating lunch, Anna's mom said, "Do you remember how to count the money in the pot?"

"Yes," said Anna. She emptied the pot and counted, "Five quarters, four dimes, one nickel, and five pennies."

"That's right. I want to give you the money in the blue pot," said her mom.

"Why? I'm your daughter and I liked helping you," said Anna.

Her mom smiled and said, "That is certainly true. But I am still giving you the money in the pot. You were honest. You did not ask me for it. You showed me the money and then you put it all back."

Anna asked, "Why did you have the money in the pot?"

Her mom said, "To save it for a special occasion, and a chance to buy a fancy, sparkly, purple yoyo is certainly a special occasion. So I decided to give you the money in the pot."

Anna ran over and gave her mom a big hug. "Doesn't all the money add up to one dollar and 75 cents? I only need one dollar and 50 cents," Anna said.

"Anna, you added it up right. You can have it all," her mom said.

Anna put the four quarters, four dimes, one nickel and five pennies into the big, pink piggy bank. She shook the piggy bank and it made a lot of noise, plus it was quite a bit heavier. She put one quarter back in her mom's blue pot when she was not looking. Then she put the pot back into the cupboard.

Anna smiled and wondered when her mom would find her surprise.

$1.50 + $3.50 = $5.00 = Yoyo!

Anna's mom said, "You have enough money for your yoyo. Would you like to go to
Mr. Jones's General Store?"

"Yes!" shouted Anna.

31

13. The Yoyo and the Piggy Bank

"Anna, you need to bring your piggy bank to the store. Is it too heavy to carry?" asked her mom.

"No, I can carry it. Listen to all the noise it makes when I shake it," said Anna. "How do I get the money out?"

"That is a lot of noise. Thanks for reminding me to get the key for the piggy bank. Do you see that lock on the bottom? The key should open it," said her mom. She put the key into her purse. Then they walked to Mr. Jones's General Store.

"My, my," said Mr. Jones. "What do we have here?"

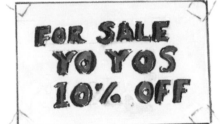

FOR SALE
YO YOS
10% OFF

32

"It's my humongous, pink piggy bank. I came to buy the fancy, sparkly, purple yoyo." said Anna. She shook the piggy bank. It made quite a noise.

Mr. Jones smiled and said, "Well, let's go find the yoyos and see if it's still there."

Anna, her mom and Mr. Jones found the yoyos. There next to the orange with gold swirls, green, sky blue, cardinal red, pink with silver swirls, lemon yellow, cloud white and silver yoyos was the fancy, sparkly, purple yoyo. The box of yoyos had a sign that said, "Sale, 10 percent off."

"What does that mean?" asked Anna.

"You're in luck, Anna," said her mom. "*Sale* means it costs less money. *Ten percent off* means you save ten cents on every dollar."

"Ten cents is one dime. The yoyo was five dollars. Does that mean I save five dimes?" asked Anna.

"Exactly!" said Mr. Jones.

"Then I have extra money," said Anna.

"Do you want to spend it?" asked her mom.

"No. I want to save it for something special," said Anna. Anna picked up the fancy, sparkly, purple yoyo, her favorite color. "I'd like to buy this purple yoyo."

"A good choice. Let's go to the counter with the cash register," said Mr. Jones.

Anna put the fancy, sparkly, purple yoyo and the humongous, pink piggy bank on the counter. Her mom got the key out of her purse. "Can you unlock the piggy bank with the key, Anna?" asked her mom.

"Yes, I can do it!" said Anna.

Anna turned the lock. Out poured the 27 coins she had earned. There were five pennies, one nickel, nine dimes, ten quarters, one half-dollar, and one dollar coin. Anna made five stacks. Each stack equalled one dollar.

34

Anna's mom wondered where the other quarter was. She did not ask.

Mr. Jones said, "You have too much money. I only need four dollars and 50 cents. What coins do you want to give me?"

Anna gave Mr. Jones the dollar coin, ten quarters, nine dimes, one nickel and the five pennies. She locked the bank. Anna put the 50-cent coin back into the piggy bank.

Mr. Jones gave Anna a receipt for four dollars and 50 cents for the fancy, sparkly, purple yoyo. He gave her a paper that showed yoyo tricks. Anna and her mom walked outside. Her mom carried the big, pink piggy bank. Anna had the purple yoyo on her middle finger.

"I am so excited. I have my own fancy, sparkly, purple yoyo," said Anna. She was very happy. She was proud she earned the money to buy it.

"Let's look at the yoyo directions," said her mom. There was a picture showing the *around the world* trick. Anna tried it. It was not easy. Her mom helped her get started.

When Anna could do it, she asked her mom, "May I go over to Jackson's house?"

Her mom smiled and said, "Certainly!"

Anna hurried to show Jackson her new fancy, sparkly, purple yoyo. Then she showed him how she could make it go *around the world*.

Anna and Jackson decided to learn new yoyo tricks together. They knew her mom and Mr. Jones could show them yoyo tricks. They showed their friends. Anna and Jackson said, "We'll help you save and get yoyos, too."

And imagine Anna's mom's surprise when she looked in her blue pot!

Add "L" to "earn" and you have "Learn"!

1. Anna's goal was to get a yoyo. Do you have something special you'd like to have?
2. Anna earned money in many ways. What way was the hardest?
3. What was the most fun?
4. What are some of the yoyo tricks? Which one would you like to learn?
5. Do you have a piggy bank or another place to save money?
6. What was the largest coin that Anna and Jackson earned? Which was the smallest Anna earned?
7. What president was on the nickel? On the half-dollar?
8. What is the name of your state? What year was your state on the quarter?
9. What was different about the dollar coin Mr. Clemens gave Anna and the one he gave Jackson?
10. What does *sale* mean? What would you have done with the extra money?
11. What surprise did Anna hide for her mom?

About the Author

Susan Werner Thoresen has educated groups of all ages on financial literacy—as a cable TV host, school board member, planning consultant and financial adviser. Sue's dad, Clem Werner, was a lawyer and small-town banker who gave his kids Iowa corn banks to teach them the value of saving coins. She enjoyed the mentorship of Else Holmelund Minarik, author of the Little Bear books, and received a National Endowment of the Humanities fellowship at the University of Iowa. She is a graduate of Smith College and Syracuse Unversity, MPA. Sue and her husband Bob live in Portsmouth, New Hampshire, and have two children and four grandchildren who were born after the third draft of this book!

About the Illustrator

Keith Eveland has had a lifelong passion for art including illustration, oil painting, watercolor and sculpture. Keith's mother was a landscape and portrait painter. His enthusiasm and creativity can be seen in the illustrations in this book. He lives in Rye, New Hampshire, with his partner Trish. He has two daughters and three granddaughters. Keith enjoys his retirement from his prior life as a pediatric dentist.